MURDER MYSTERY

1

SHAMS-UZ-ZOHA

AURAQ

Printed in the Islamic Republic of Pakistan.
Printed: November, 2020
Edition: 1st
ISBN: 978-969-749-046-2
Price: Rs 800 PKR, $08 US

AURAQ PUBLICATIONS

ISLAMABAD, PAKISTAN

raabta@auraqpublications.com.pk | +92-300-0571-530
www.auraqpublications.com.pk | @AuraqPublications

ISBN : 978-969-749-046-2

Specials thanks to:

- MY SISTER

Sherza Mohtashim

- MY MOTHER

Anis Khatoon

- MY AUNT

Humaira Gazan

Author Note

It doesn't matter how young you are. The thing that matter is the creativity your mind holds, the powerful thoughts that are hiding deep inside you, the spirit you have for what you want and your creativity should spread like stars in the sky, Infinite and never-ending.

MURDER MYSTERY

This is a story about a Famous Magician 'Andrew Godwin' who was killed while the performance of his trick. Detective 'Thomas Rockford reopened the case and the research begin.

Contents

CHPATER 01

WHODUNIT

Magicians perform illusions to confound and amuse their audience. They enter the world of magic without any fear. A year ago a famous magician "Andrew Godwin" enter the same world of magic and was killed while performing a dangerous magic trick 'the car on fire' in the city of brukland. He was thirty five years old, bossy and a very well known magician of his time. He wasn't married because he was so busy in creating his carrer. He use to say, "Never ever throw in the towel, Never let your competitors defeat you, one defeat and you are lost for a life time". He wasn't familiar with the word failure. The mystery of his murder wasn't solved because the detective who was solving this mystery was killed. Many people believe that he was killed because he was near the killer. But as it is said, 'People know how to make up things from a small talk'. Later "Thomas Rockford" reopen the case and the research begin. Thomas was not a professional detective. He was 23 years old but he wanted to solve this case. Olivia Marple was the one to blame. Oliva was Andrew's assistant who was assisting her magic trick. It was observed that after the trick Andrew's body was not found maybe it was all burned or maybe a piece of the puzzle was missing. Thomas handed over the case to detective "August Spade" and "Sam Holmes". After two weeks of the research, August was killed. While the research was still going on by Sam Holmes. Exactly after four weeks of the research, Sam was also killed. Thomas Rockford wanted to know the mystery behind it so he decided to solve the case by himself. When Thomas started the research detective Jim Hercule also joined him. The research made by Sam and August was proving Olivia guilty. But however, Thomas thought that Olivia is not the one to be blamed. At night Thomas went back home while Jim was in the research lab doing the research. When Thomas reached home he saw an envelope lying outside his house, when he opened the envelope he saw photos of the incident. He perceived that Olivia was not there while Andrew was performing his trick. On the other hand, someone knocked the door of the research lab, Jim opened the door and found a disk lying on the floor. When he played the disk he noticed that it was the footage of the incident. He also observed that Olivia was missing and the door of the car was not opening, Andrew was shouting for help but Olivia wasn't there. Next day Jim and Thomas told each other everything but the question that comes in their mind was,

"Who is sending us these photos and footage? and Where was Olivia during the incident?"

They went to Olivia's house and when they asked her that where was she?

she replied,"Andrew asked me to leave for

the reason that I knew he wasn't all set for the trick constantly we had a spat and he asked me to leave".

"If you knew he wasn't ready so why didn't you stopped him?" Jim asked her.

 She replied angrily," I did, I did but he doesn't eavesdrop to me."

 Jim said, "I think we are wasting our time this is just an accident, not a murder."

 while they were discussing this Olivia took the phone out of her pocket and handed over the phone to Thomas. Thomas stared at the phone curiously.

Olivia exhaled and said," This is Andrew's phone and this is a murder, not an incident and please dont stop the investigation."

They took the phone and left. They checked the call history of the phone and found the last call Andrew did was to a person named Philip Dupin. They started research on Philip and found that he is also a famous magician. For the investigation, they went to him and told him about Andrew. All of a sudden he started crying and

said," Andrew my dear friend, yeah I heard about him, we were best friends but death never spare anybody."

Jim looked at him cleverly and said," So you were best friends huh! Then why did you killed him?"

Philip was shocked and num, He was blank because he wasn't expecting this question. Jim repeated his question.

Philip replied nervously, "I-I-I didn't kill him. Why would I do that?"

"You can lie but your mouth cannot, the crocodile tears can tell me a lot about you" said Jim.

He wiped his tears, "I didn't killed him"

Why are you so nervous, I am just joking or

might say playing a trick on you" Jim said.

Then after a while, Thomas asked him," Why did Andrew call you before going to the performance?"

He replied," He called me because he wanted to know whether I will attend the performance or not?"

"So did you attend?" Jim asked.

One after another question and each question was making Philip nervous maybe he was worried that why detectives are doubting him well this time

he confidently replied," No! I was not in the

town."

Jim looked at him with having a smile on his face and asked," OK then tell us where were you?"

"I was in California" he replied.

Jim teasingly said," I love Califorina by the way I was also there two weeks ago."

"Glad to know that" he replied. Philip's hesitation was not giving good signals to the detectives.

However they left but still doubt was there in their minds. When the detectives reaches at their house, Jim was so tired that he slept. After some time he heard some voice coming from the kitchen. He took his gun and moved silently towards the kitchen but he found no one except for the glass lying on the floor as he bows down to picked the glass he heard some voices coming from his room without having a second thought he ran towards his room and saw that the window of his room was broken and all the evidence they collected were missing meanwhile Thomas received a call from Olivia.

She was sounding so afraid and said," Thomas please help me, he'll kill me."

the call ended. Thomas immediately took his car and drove towards her house as fast as he could. When he was on his way

he again received a call," Thomas listen-listen to me I want to tell you that Andrew..."

From the back, the person said," Tell you what? Olivia!?"

The call ended again. Now he started driving faster. At last he reached at Olivia's house. He tried to look for Olivia everywhere at last she was sitting in the backyard. When he went near her he saw that she was dead. Olivia was DEAD. Before the police came he took Olivia's phone and left. He called Jim to the research lab and told him everything. Jim also told him about what happened. Thomas was thinking about the voice he heard in the back when Olivia called him. However next day both the detectives went to attend Olivia's funeral. While they were standing in the corner a lady came to them and said," I am Kate Marple, Olivia's mother."

"I am sorry about what happened." Thomas said.

Kate replied," No one can change what happened, first Andrew died while performing the trick than Olivia died while knowing who was the killer."

Jim gazed at her shockingly and said," How do you know that she knew who was the killer?".

She was num for a second and then replied," Before calling Thomas she called me actually, I was out of the city so I asked her to call Thomas as his house was near and I was not having your number, Thomas."

Jim asked curiously, "Did she gave any information about the killer?"

"No, the call was disconnected and excuse me because I have to serve other guests" and she left.

At once Jim thought about Olivia's phone. After attending the funeral when they reached the research lab Jim straight away opened the call history of Olivia's phone and found that before calling Thomas she didn't called Kate. Jim and Thomas were surprised that why Kate lied to them. Many questions were revolving in their minds that who sent those proof? who stole those evidence? Does Philip lied to us? why kate lied to us?

CHPATER 02
RED HERRING

The mystery was becoming complicated at every coming moment. At night Thomas was judgmental about the assert he heard once Olivia called him. That voice seems so familiar to him. He was saying to himself again and again," Thomas just think a little harder.". He was lying on the couch and all of a sudden jumped saying,

"I remember the voice, I reminisce the voice."

He peered in the mirror and asked himself," Do I really remember the voice?"

Because the person he remembers was no one else but Philip. Jim was also doing the research on Kate Marple and found that Kate is the step-mother of Olivia. Her actual mother, Julia died in a car crash. Next morning when they met at the research lab Jim told Thomas about Kate. When Thomas told him about Philip he said,

"Ok but we can't doubt anyone on the basis of guesses Thomas."

A thought hit Thomas mind and he went to Olivia's house to check the CCTV footage and discerned that the footage of that day was missing. He came back home as he was frustrated because they didn't even get the starting piece of the puzzle. He was asking himself,

"Am I not near the killer because Olivia was killed knowing about the murderer, August and Sam was also killed maybe they were near the slayer. If I was even a step close to him he would have killed me."

He heard his doorbell. When he opened the gate he saw a letter lying on the ground. He opened the letter but it was blank. He thought that why would anybody send a blank letter to him. He tried everything to see what is written inside the letter but failed at last he put the letter above the flame of the candle and the writing appear. His hands started shaking after reading the letter, it was written," Slant of demise is on its way to you." He called jim and said,

'I sense that we must bring this investigation to an end."

Jim asked him to meet him first in the

morning. He was not proficient to catnap the whole night because of the letter. In the morning he told everything to Jim. Jim read the letter and said,"

Pay attention to me Thomas this is truly a stupid letter. You are a detective, not an adolescent so don't be anxious, nothing will happen. And as a detective you should know how to swim again the tides"

 He was dispelled frightened but pretented to be robust. Jim took the letter and sent Thomas home for the reason that he tin static catch a glimpse of a nightmare in his eyes. Meanwhile Jim has burdened the delve in the lab so after an hour he became fatigued and thought of going out in the cafe. He took the letter and the phone with him so he can bottle up the last touches on the inquiries in the cafe. He thought of grabbing the coffee, he went to grab the coffee and left the research on the table. When he came back he detected Olivia's phone was gone but the letter was immobile in attendance. On his direction recede to the inquiries lab he saw an old hut, on the outside, of the hut it was written, " *FUTURE TELLER HELEN.*" Jim went inside the hut as he entered he saw an old lady sitting on a wooden chair.

The lady said," Lad of David Johnson, Jim Hercule you were destined to arrive here."

He was surprised, he asked the lady, "How do you know my and my father's name?"

 She had a slight smile on her face and replied, "Expensive! your hand watch is pricey, beautiful! coffins they are beautiful. They must have cost you a daylight robbery. I see you are following the footsteps of your father. Son this beauty does not matter your, heart needs to be beautiful and expensive. Son the weather is getting bad go and hide under your hut."

Jim replied, 'Strom is a teacup for me' he

passed the epistle to her," Can you tell me whose calligraphy is this."

She glanced at the letter, "So you are solving a mystery. Sometimes truth is in front of your eyes you just have to focus."

"Can you please be a little straight forward and just tell me whose handwriting is this and I will pay you?"

After hearing the question of Jim she was dishearted, "Money? Money cannot buy everything in this universe. Save your money for a rainy day and I cannot help because I am a future teller not a letter detector."

Jim scowled at her heatedly, "I assume that I must leave."

Helen stopped him by saying, "Don't you want to know anything about yourself?"

He leans forward and said, "No! Because I love mysteries and yes also I love rainy days."

She laughed," Yes! Life is a mystery but stash one thing in mind that magicians create the magic, magic wasn't instinctive itself."

She smiled cleverly. He furiously took the letter and went back to the research lab.

Thomas was also in the research lab.

Jim asked him that if he is ok?

"Yes I am fine now" he said.

Someone knocked on the door of the lab. Jim opened the door, a tall lady with golden hair and blue eyes was standing,

"Who are you?" Jim asked her.

She smiled and replied, "Christina, detective Christina Jeniffer and I am here to help with the case." She was having a black case in her hand.

"Jim let her in" Thomas said.

She walked in a stunt.

She introduced herself "I am Christina Jennifer. I have been solving this case since the last six months and wanted to share some information that I have collected which might help you with the case." She opened the black case and said, "So shall I start?" she asked in a friendly way

 "Yes sure" Jim replied while sitting on the chair.

She took the picture of Andrew, subsequently paste it on the wall and said, "Andrew Godwin was an infamous magician, killed during the implementation of his trick, the body was not found hence we don't know that if he died or not. After that is August Spade, the detective hired by detective Thomas Rockford, Killed on 21st January. Next is Sam Holmes also a detective hired by Thomas Rockford, Murdered on 17 of July. Moving on to Olivia Marple assistant of Andrew, Died on 11th of September. Last but not the least Philip Dupin a clever, smart and intelligent also he was a great competitor of Andrew Godwin."

"Competitor?" Jim said anxiously and Christina replied,

"Yes, they were competitors and according to the research Sam, August, Olivia died at night, by focusing on the dates you will note that on these dates Lunar eclipse occurs so the killer can be Lunatic."

 "We are not sure miss Christina Jennifer because he might be a son of a gun." Jim replied.

 Thomas examined the research made by Christina and said, "Yes we are not sure but by the way welcome to our detective team."

CHPATER 03
A GONG SHOW

Everyone was doing the research. Christina came and handed the USB to Thomas.

He asked her,"I beg your pardon? This is?

She replied, "Just play this and you'll know".

He played the USB and found that it was the footage of Olivia's rehearsing area where she received a call and started shouting on the phone. Thomas asked Jim that this is his responsibility to discover the individual she was talking to. Jim realized that he has misplaced her phone in the cafe but after then he recalled that her call history was in the laptop so he opened her call history and found that on that day she received the call from Philip. Another prove against Philip Dupin. After that, they went to see Philip.

When they went there his assistant John Ray clogged them and said, "Sir is busy in practice."

The detectives were busy in talking with his assistant, Christina took advantage of the circumstance and entered from the back gate. She saw that Philip was lying on the sofa and wasn't busy in practice. She was surprised. She wanted to ask Philip but left with many questions in her mind. Jim heeded that Christina wasn't there so he called her. Christina asked him to get here to the lab. When they reached the lab Christina told them everything she axiom. They were flabbergasted that why Philip's assistant lied to them now at this point everything was against Philip. But they might be barking up the wrong tree. At night when Christina was sleeping she received a text, "Masquerade party, PC Hotel at sharp 12." She looked at the time it was already 11:30. After that, she acknowledged another text " If you want to know who is the KILLER than be there at the party." Without any second thought, she called Jim and Thomas and told them to meet at the main gate of PC Hotel with masks.

When they reach at the masquerade party everyone was wearing masks except for the lady sitting on the chair and she was no one else but Helen. Jim looked at her surprisingly he asked Thomas and Christina

to look for the person who texted her and

he went to Helen, tapped her shoulder,

"What are you doing here?" he asked.

She looked at him, smiled and said, "Jim

glad to see you, well you want the Host to

be missing?"

"But..." Jim was going to pose a question

but Helen ignored him and saunter away.

He knew that incredible odd is up for a

grab now. He adage Helen moving upstairs

so he followed her. She went inside the

room and locked the door. Jim wanted to

know who else is inside the room as he was hearing voices so he stared from the keyhole.

Dejectedly Jim was not proficient to see the guy as his flipside was at Jim, "Helen I can't do this." the man said.

Someone tapped Jim's shoulder as Jim recede Christina was standing there, "What are you doing here?" She asked.

Jim glared at her furiously but noiselessly said," Can you please low down your intonation? And let me see."

As he looked to glance from the keyhole

Helen opened the door, Jim fell in her feet. She looked at him and said, "Jim? Are you following me?"

"No actually Christina was finding the washroom so I was helping her" He replied by taking a step back.

Helen grimaced at him curiously, " Straight then left" she replied.

" Come honey I will take you to the washroom." Jim said.

He pretended that he is taking Christina to the washroom but as Helen went downstairs he asked Christina to go down and search for the person who texted her. She wanted to ask from him that what is going on but as he was furious so she left. Jim went in Helen's room but there was no one. The person in the room clearly disappeared. He looked for him all over the room but he was nowhere to be found.

He said to himself, "I think I am running out of steam and I am going to blow my top soon"

Jim was livid with himself as he lost this chance. In anger, he punched the wall and saw that there was a path hiding at the back of Almira.

"A hidden way, he must have gone out from here." He said to himself and went inside. Meanwhile, Thomas aphorism Philip but he wasn't sure that he is Philip for the reason that it was a masquerade party.

Thomas pretended to be his admirer and went to him, "Is this Philip Dupin? I presage the Philip Dupin."

The gentleman replied, "Any Doubt about it?".

"No Sir, I am a big fan of yours."

Now Thomas knew that he is Philip.

Philip excused him by saying, "Excuse me

for now and enjoy the party."

Thomas followed him, he went to the restroom. Thomas waited for him outside but after a sustained time as he didn't come out, Thomas went inside and noticed that Philip wasn't there. He was heading out but he saw Philip's ring laying under the sink. When he picked the ring he observed that the tiles were not present there and when he moved those tiles he also found a small hidden way. Christina was finding them everywhere and saw a lad that looks so familiar to her.

As she went near him the person on the

stage said, "It's time for all of you to join the dance floor."

He looked at Christina and offer her for a dance as they started dancing Christina tried to remove his mask but failed,

"Are you enjoying the party" He asked.

His voice also seems familiar to Christina "Honestly this is a Gong show" she replied.

The young man laughed, "Same here"

"What do you do?" She asked.

He nervously replied "I am spilling the bean, I am out of work."

She wasn't expecting this reply "Really? you don't look like one maybe because you speak with a plum in your mouth."

He laughed, "Thank you, by the way, you look pretty too miss boss lady"

She smiled, "And you look like a dead ringer"

He excused Christina and left. Meanwhile, when Thomas reached the middle of his path he saw a person sitting on the stone and Thomas said, "Don't move otherwise I will shoot and remove your mask." As he removed his mask he was Jim,

"Jim? What are you doing here?" Thomas asked him.

Jim and Thomas told each other everything and start to move again to see where the path ends.

After a while, Christina receives a call from Jim, "Come out we are waiting for you on the main gate." Jim said.

Christina went out and asked them that where were they? They told Christina everything, Christina also told them about the young man. After that they all went to home from the party. It was 5am. They all were at their home but couldn't slumber after what happened at the party.

Next day they met at the research lab, "I am sure Helen has a link with this case." alleged Jim.

Christina was silent and was still thinking about the Young man she met at the party,

"It's a catch-22 situation." said Thomas.

"Yes it is but we are detectives and it is our duty to solve this mystery." Cristina said.

Jim started laughing and said, "Mystery isn't the problem, the problem is finding the killer Find..Find with a capital F!"

"Ok let us get back to work guys" Thomas said pointing towards the chairs.

CHPATER 04
A HARD NUT TO CRACK

While everyone was doing the research Thomas felt stale and went home. As he reached home he went to the washroom to get fresh. On the other hand, Christina contacted the IT company to recognize the person who texted her.

Meanwhile she received another text from the same number,' One of you will die today so lets me check the guess of miss detective that can she guess who will die today? The countdown starts 5, 4, 3...'

She looked at Jim and said, 'Jim, Thomas is in danger.'

He didn't know what was going on, 'But why? How? When? I mean...' He asked.

Christina handed the phone to him. He read the text and derived towards his house as fast as he possibly can.

Thomas came out and was drying his hair,

he read a note written on the mirror, "Didn't I told you that slant of demise is on its way and now he has reached your door so look back."

As he looked back a bullet hits his forehead and he died at the spot. The individuals heard the voice of the bullet and called the Police. Before the police, Christina and Jim reached to his flat and saw him lifeless on the floor plus the writing on the mirror was exactly like the writing on the letter. They left as the police arrived. Christina hypocrisy stays longer for the reason that no one knows the subsequent step of the Killer therefore she called the IT company and requested them to provide her with the information as soon as possible. The murder of Thomas was a cumbersome shock for the detectives.

When it was investigated that if anyone saw anybody entering Thomas's house all denied, "No, we bearly heard the voice of the bullet." They replied.

Jim said," He is one of the hard nuts to break."

Christina was waiting for the call from the IT company, 'Life is not a bowl of cherries Jim.'

she replied, ' We can't trust anybody here not even ourselves.'

Jim drag the chair and sat beside her, ' You mean I am not trustworthy' he said, ' Wait, I think Killer is a ghost don't you think so.'

She bang her head against the desk in frustration, ' Can you think out of the box' she replied, 'Please this is a serious matter.'

Jim stood from his chair, ' SERIOUS huh!?' he said, 'Then spill the bean out Christina'.

She also stood from the chair, 'What bean Jim?' she asked, ' What are you saying.'

Jim rolled his eyes, ' Why are you helping

me?' he asked, 'Why have you even joined us.'

She was shocked, ' Are you in your senses Jim?' she asked, ' What type of questions are these?'

Jim punched the desk, 'I am a detective and you are in my doubt circle right now.' he said, 'so answer me.'

Christina was blank because she wasn't expecting these questions, ' Because I wanted to help' she replied, ' I wanted to slove this mystery and wait tell me why are you solving this mystery, Jim Hercule?'

Jim sat on the chair, 'Ah, same.' Jim replied, ' Actually we shouldn't be doubting each other.'

Christina sat beside him, 'See now can you please shut your stupid questions' Christina said, 'and get back to the investigation.'

Christina received the call from IT company ' We found the information about that person they said, 'Please come and collect it.'

Christina quoted "Found it" she said, ' I will be there any minute.'

She left and when she reached there the girl

handed the information to her. The person who texted her was no one else but Helen. Without wasting a second she called Jim and asked him to be at Helen's house in 5 minutes. When Jim reached there Christina told him everything. As they went in, Helen was sitting on the sofa.

They handed the information to Helen, 'What is this' Christina said, 'Can't believe that you are the one.'

Helen looked at the paper, stood, moved back and took the Gun out from the drawer. Jim and Christina also took their guns and point towards Helen.

Helen pointed the gun towards Jim, ' I am not the Killer ' she said, ' I was forced to do this,Trust me Jim.'

Christina moved one step closer to Helen, 'Ok calm down, we won't harm you.' she said very politely, 'Just tell us Helen who is the Killer?'

Helen was shaking,'The person who forced me and who killed everyone is'

Before she could spill the name out of her mouth someone shot on her neck and she died at the spot. Christina ran towards Helen and Jim ran toward the shooter. She took Helen's phone for investigation, called the police from the telephone and left.

 When Jim reached the research lab Christina gave him the glass of water, 'What happened?' she asked, ' Did you saw him?'.

He sat on the chair, 'No he ran' he replied.

 Christina showed him the phone, ' Well I got Helen's phone' she said, 'Maybe it will help.'

Jim took the phone, ' It will surely help' he replied, ' Let me check the call history and messages.'

He opened the call history of the phone, empty then he opened the messages, empty,

'Useless' she said, 'Just throw it away.'

 Jim was continuously looking at the phone

"Wait it is not useless.' he said ' I got

something.'

CHPATER 05

THE MURDER MYSTERY ENDS

Finally, the mystery came to an end. Jim opened the phone's gallery, there was a video of the killer accepting his crime.

"We were not barking up the wrong tree," said Jim.

Christina called the police for the reason that

she sensed going alone there would be exceptionally dangerous. They went to his mansion. Christina crossed her fingers. They checked every room but he was nowhere to be found. They traced his phone and as his phone was traced, they went there. It was a delightful undersized hut in the core of the tall mountains. They searched everywhere at last he was sitting on the edge of the mountain reading a book. Christina and Jim went near him,

He was countinuously reading the book, 'finally, finally you are here, I was in the offing waiting for so long' he said, 'Even I have completed my novel.'

He closed his book and put it beside him. Jim

glanced at the book and the name of the book was " THE MURDER MYSTERY".

Everyone was pointing the gun towards him, 'Don't move Philip Dupin' Christina said, ' Let the Law take your decision.'

He laughed, ' But Christina the law of my life says that handing myself to the law of the world is not my style.'

Jim was surprised to see his attitude, 'Make the long story short' He said, 'And don't act smart'.

He stood up, 'Don't you want to know who sent you those proves?.' He replied. 'I did, so you might doubt Olivia but you didn't so I also stole those proves."

Jim moves one step closer to him, ' Why did you kill her and everyone'

He replied, "You missed the boat."

No one was expecting this kind of response from him.

He smiled, 'GOODBYE' and he jumped from the mountain.

Everyone ran towards him but it was too late. Christina opened the book he was reading and on the first page it was written,

'I am leaving without answering your questions that why I killed Thomas, Olivia, Sam, August and above all Andrew. The reason I killed Andrew was revenge, revenge for my daughter.

He killed my daughter in the facade of my own eyes. She was just 18 years old and she wanted to become the magician so she went to him. And when she became good enough in tricks, he became green with envy and in the same trick (The car on fire) he killed my daughter, locked her, she was screaming and I was begging for her life as I was locked inside the room and I saw my daughter burning, dying through the windows of the room. I was helpless and he was laughing, he was spinning the keys in his fingers. I tried to take help from the law but I was poor so the law didn't help me. I was left with no other option that is why I killed him. Then I killed all those who knew about me; Olivia, Sam, August, Helen or who was even near me like Thomas. To me, this world is nothing but evil, and my own evil just happened to come out because of the circumstances. I am so sorry but I wanted justice so I killed him and I was afraid so killed everyone one by one. I am not bad and I am not guilty. GOODBYE finally THE MURDER MYSTERY SOLVED..' Christina closed the book.

END OF MYSTERY 1

www.ingramcontent.com/pod-product-compliance
Lightning Source LLC
Chambersburg PA
CBHW051450140726
47987CB00006B/2626